DAISY SAVES THE DAY

For Alice with love

༄

First published 2014 by Walker Books Ltd
87 Vauxhall Walk, London SE11 5HJ

2 4 6 8 10 9 7 5 3 1

© 2014 Shirley Hughes

The right of Shirley Hughes to be identified as author/illustrator
of this work has been asserted by her in accordance with
the Copyright, Designs and Patents Act 1988

This book has been typeset in Filosofia

Printed in China

British Library Cataloguing in Publication Data:
a catalogue record for this book is
available from the British Library

ISBN 978-1-4063-4899-6

www.walker.co.uk

DAISY SAVES THE DAY

Shirley Hughes

WALKER BOOKS
AND SUBSIDIARIES
LONDON • BOSTON • SYDNEY • AUCKLAND

ONCE, NOT SO VERY LONG AGO, there was a girl called Daisy Dobbs. She had a mum and two little twin brothers, and they were very hard up.

At school the teacher said that Daisy was exceptionally bright. She could read and do beautiful handwriting and reckon figures in her head.

But often, when Mum was out at work, Daisy had to stay at home and look after the twins. She longed to have some books of her own to read, but they were too poor to buy any. Instead, she made up wonderful stories and told them to the twins at bedtime.

Then the sad day came when Mum told Daisy that it was time for her to leave school altogether and go out to work too.

"I've got you a job as a scullery maid," she said. "It's in a very nice home owned by two ladies, the Misses Simms, very refined. There's a cook and a parlour maid so the work won't be too hard. And you'll be living in, get your keep and all."

"You mean I won't be living at home with you and Tommy and Billy any more?" asked Daisy sadly.

"No, but you'll have your own uniform, a half-day off every week and one whole Sunday a month."

So one spring morning, very early, Mum left the twins with a neighbour and she and Daisy set out from their home on the far outskirts of London, carrying all Daisy's belongings in a small suitcase.

It was a very long journey into the city, first by train and then a weary walk from the station. At last they arrived at the house where the Misses Simms lived. It was a tall house in a row of other tall houses, with lace curtains in every window except for the attic.

They went down the basement steps to the back door and rang the bell.

The parlour maid answered. "So, you're the new scullery maid," she said, looking Daisy up and down. "Bit young for the job aren't you?"

"She's a very good worker," said Mum anxiously.

"You'd better start right away then. There's plenty to do, I can tell you."

Daisy was very sad to say goodbye to Mum. But she bravely managed not to cry.

Soon she was wearing a cap and a big apron over her blue cotton dress and was set to work washing dishes, scouring saucepans and peeling potatoes for the cook.

Miss Jessie and Miss Margaret Simms were quite old. They sat in the front parlour by a big coal fire. When they wanted something they rang the bell for the parlour maid, whose name was Ellen. She did a lot of running up and down the stairs which made her cross. But not as cross as Cook, who toiled endlessly over the big hot kitchen range, preparing meals and baking scones and cakes.

Daisy was not very good at housework but she worked very hard. She swept the stairs and carried buckets of coal for the fires and helped with the laundry. She scrubbed the front doorstep and polished the knocker till it shone.

"This looks very nice, Daisy," said Miss Jessie encouragingly as she and Miss Margaret were setting out for their morning walk.

"Thank you, ma'am," Daisy replied, remembering to bob a curtsey.

At the end of each day she was very tired.
After supper Ellen and Cook sat chatting by
the kitchen fire. Daisy knew that they wanted
to have a grown-up gossip, so she did not try
to join them. Instead she went up to her little
attic bedroom and huddled under her blanket,
missing Mum and the twins and longing for her
day off. Even when that came she could not
afford the fare home.

But now summer was on the way and there was great excitement in the quiet house. The Misses Simms' niece, Miss Mabel Simms, was coming for a visit all the way from America.

On the day of her arrival they were all in the hall to greet her. She was tall and untidy and wore her hat on the back of her head.

"I sure am glad to meet you all!" she said, and shook hands with all the servants, even Daisy.

She was a very friendly lady.

One day when Daisy was bringing in the coal for the parlour fire, Miss Mabel asked if she could read.

"Oh yes, Miss." She looked longingly at the bookcase. "When I was at school it was my favourite thing in all the world."

"Me too. I'll ask my aunts if you can borrow one of these from time to time."

After this Daisy did not feel so lonely. Some of the books were too difficult for her to read, but others had pictures and they were her favourites. She took them up to her room and pored over them whenever she could. She specially loved stories about princesses, kings and queens.

That summer was a very special one because the new King, George V, was going to be crowned. Miss Mabel had timed her visit specially to see the coronation procession. Daisy went out into the streets whenever she could, to see the Union Jack flags flying everywhere and red, white and blue streamers wound around the lampposts.

Miss Jessie and Miss Margaret Simms, though they were very patriotic, considered that all this was a little vulgar. Their house was the only one in the street that remained undecorated. Daisy thought that was a sad shame.

When the great day came, the three ladies set out very early. They had been invited to watch the procession by some friends whose house overlooked the route.

Cook and Ellen had the day off and were going out too. But Daisy was to be left all alone. They told her that she was too young to go out among all the crowds and she was to stay indoors all day.

After they had gone, Daisy wandered slowly upstairs to her room. From her little attic window she could see the people celebrating in the street below, and she could just hear the brass band playing in the park. It all seemed like a wonderful story-book adventure, and she wanted to be part of it. She watched for a long time.

Then she had a good idea. She went downstairs and found the spare washing line and some clothes pegs. She looked out some white pillowcases and blue dish cloths, but she needed something red. The only red things Daisy could find were the scarlet flannel bloomers that the older Misses Simms wore in cold weather.

Daisy took them upstairs to her room
and pegged them firmly on the line,
alternating red, white and blue.

Then she tied one end of the line to her window catch and let the other drop. It hung right down in front of the house, fluttering festively in the breeze.

Passers-by laughed and pointed when they saw it. They looked up and waved at Daisy and she waved back. She felt she was part of the celebrations at last.

But when the Misses Simms came home that evening and saw their red bloomers hanging out for all to see, they were gravely displeased. Daisy would have been dismissed on the spot and sent home in disgrace – if it had not been for Miss Mabel.

She thought the whole thing was a huge joke and managed to persuade her aunts to give Daisy another chance. "She is only young, and she wanted to join in," Miss Mabel said.

After this, Daisy was kept in disgrace. Ellen and Cook hardly spoke to her except to order her about, and they gave her all the nasty chores to do. When her day's work was done she was too tired even to read.

One Sunday the three ladies went out
visiting. Ellen had the evening off,
and Cook was settled in her chair
in front of the kitchen fire.

Daisy went miserably up to
her room.

It was chilly up there.
She curled up under her blanket,
shed a few tears and went off to sleep.

When she awoke it was dark.
There was a strange smell in
the room — a smell of burning.

Daisy scrambled up, flung open her bedroom door and ran downstairs.

The hall was full of smoke. When she reached the kitchen there was Cook, slumped fast asleep in her chair, and the dish cloths which she had hung near the kitchen range to dry had caught fire. They were already ablaze.

Daisy shook Cook awake, and together they ran to fill jugs and saucepans with water from the kitchen sink. They sloshed it over the flames. There was a horrible sound and the smoke made them cough, but they had caught the fire just in time.

Daisy had saved the day.

"Thank heavens you discovered it when you did," said Miss Jessie when the ladies returned.

"You are a brave girl, Daisy," said Miss Margaret.

"You can say that again!" said Miss Mabel.

The next morning Daisy was summoned to the parlour where all three ladies were assembled.

"We've been discussing how to reward you for your prompt and plucky action," Miss Jessie told her. "Without it this house would have been badly damaged, perhaps even with loss of life. So my niece, Miss Mabel, has come up with this suggestion which I hope will be acceptable to you. As you don't seem very well suited to domestic work…"

"I've tried my best, Miss," said Daisy anxiously.

"Of course, we know that. But it seems to me that you are better at reading than at polishing and scrubbing. And we thought that as a reward, your mother might see fit to accept a sum of money from us to pay for your schooling."

"You mean I could go home, Miss?"

"Yes," said Miss Mabel. "You will be able to attend school again regularly, and if you do well you might go to the grammar school next year."

"So I won't be in service any more?" gasped Daisy.

"Just that, Daisy," said Miss Mabel, smiling broadly. "If you agree, that is!"

For a moment Daisy was speechless. She was thinking about going home to Mum and the twins, and being able to learn and read again, and tell stories to them.

Her nose turned bright pink.

"Oh, yes please, Miss!" she said at last.

THE END

Come down every morning Feeling Really Well!

IT is astonishing how many people begin the day wearily, and go through it without zest, when they have no ailment that calls for "Doctor's advice." The vast majority are simply suffering from constipation, and only PURGEN is needed to put them right and keep them so. Drastic drugs may remedy constipation for a time, but in the end they always do more harm than good.

PURGEN

is at once mild and effective, and its effectiveness does not wear off by prolonged use. Ladies will find this a particularly agreeable medicine, both for themselves and for their children.

Of leading Chemists and Stores.

Price **1/1½d.** per Box,

or Sample and Booklet Free from N. & T. KIRBY & Co., Ltd., 14, Newman St., Oxford St., W.

Watson's 'Argus' Reflex Camera

OF BRITISH WORKMANSHIP

AN IMPROVED PATTERN NOW READY

WATSON'S NEW 'ARGUS'

Watson's "Holostigmat" Convertible Lens

W. WATSON & SONS, Ltd.

'Meltonian' PASTE

(Black and Brown.)

Absolutely the best PASTE

POLISH

for cleaning and preserving your boots and shoes

Made by E. BROWN & SON

SOLD EVERYWHERE.